I LOVE MY BABY SISTER
(MOST OF THE TIME)

BY ELAINE EDELMAN · PICTURES BY WENDY WATSON

PUFFIN BOOKS

For my Mother and Father
—E.E.

PUFFIN BOOKS
Published by the Penguin Group
Viking Penguin Inc., 40 West 23rd Street, New York, New York 10010, U.S.A.
Penguin Books Ltd, 27 Wrights Lane, London W8 5TZ England
Penguin Books Australia Ltd., Ringwood, Victoria, Australia
Penguin Books Canada Ltd, 2801 John Street, Markham, Ontario, Canada L3R 1B4
Penguin Books (N.Z.) Ltd, 182–190 Wairau Road, Auckland 10, New Zealand

Penguin Books Ltd, Registered Offices: Harmondsworth, Middlesex, England
First published in the United States of America by Lothrop, Lee & Shepard Books 1984
Published in Picture Puffins 1985
7 9 10 8 6
Text copyright © Elaine Edelman, 1984
Illustrations copyright © Wendy Watson, 1984
All rights reserved

Manufactured in U.S.A.

Set in Galliard

Library of Congress Cataloging in Publication Data
Edelman, Elaine.   I love my baby sister (most of the time).
(Picture puffins)
Summary: A small girl looks forward to the time
when her baby sister will be big enough to play
with and be friends with.
1. Children's stories, American.   [1. Babies—
Fiction. 2. Sisters—Fiction]   I. Watson, Wendy, ill. II. Title.
PZ7.E216Iad   1985   [E]   85-574   ISBN 0 14 050.547 4

We have a new baby.

All she can say is *laa-laa, laa-laa*.
Sometimes she sings it,
so I sing along too.
She's my little sister.

She's fun to cuddle,
but I have to be careful.
My daddy says babies get hurt very easily.

But sometimes she yanks my hair,
and that hurts *me*.
I don't cry, though—
she's just a tiny baby.

Once I gave her a lollipop,

but she gave it back.

So I gave it back to her,

but she gave it back again.   So I ate it.

What a silly baby! When she's happy,
she laughs and makes funny noises.
Sometimes she makes mouth-bubbles. They're kind of sticky.

But when she's mad,

she screams worse than a hundred fire engines.

I don't like *that* at all.

She's too little to play my big-girl games.

Mostly, she just sleeps.

So I sing to her the way my daddy sings to me.

Good night, baby.

Sleep tight, baby.

Don't wake up 'til morning light, baby.

Sometimes my baby sister keeps Mother so busy

I have to jump around and holler, just to get a hug.

And when she eats, she does it so funny,
I have to wipe her nose and mouth for her.
Then, sometimes, she grabs my nose—ow!
My mother says she does that
because she loves me.

She'll be more fun
when she gets as big as me.
But then, I'll be a lot bigger too.

And I'll have to show her how to dress herself
and how to build with blocks.

We'll be friends
and hold hands
when we cross the street

and share our bikes and skates
and brush each other's hair....

And I might even let her button me
in the back, where I can't reach.

I hope my baby sister grows up soon.